c

BLACK BARON

BLACK BARON
ROBYN OPIE

**WALKER
BOOKS**

First published in Great Britain 2009 by Walker Books Ltd
87 Vauxhall Walk, London SE11 5HJ

2 4 6 8 10 9 7 5 3 1

Text © 2008 Robyn Opie

Illustrations © 2008 iStockphoto.com

This book has been typeset in Frutiger

Printed and bound in Great Britain by Clays Ltd, St Ives plc

British Library Cataloguing in Publication Data:
a catalogue record for this book is
available from the British Library

ISBN 978-1-4063-2216-3

www.walker.co.uk

To my best friend Rob.
You're a champ.

CHAPTER 1
BLACK BARON RULES

"Go, Black Baron!" I yelled.

The Baron raced across the concrete. He was almost home. We were almost champions. Again!

Then he stopped. My heart hit my shoes. Bugsy was catching up.

Man, what was wrong with the Baron? He could beat Bugsy with his feelers tied behind his back any day.

"Go, Black Baron!" yelled Jimbo.

I leant forward and hissed, "I'll call the exterminator if you don't hurry up." I didn't mean it, of course. I wouldn't hurt Black Baron for anything.

He must have heard me above the noise of the crowd. He waved one black feeler, like a victory salute, then scuttled forward, running way too fast for the out-of-form Bugsy. A huge roar went up as the Baron crossed the finishing line, a red chalk line drawn across the bottom of Rick's driveway.

"Way to go, Black Baron," I yelled, punching the air.

BLACK BARON RULZ

GO BLACK BARON!

Jimbo and I slapped our hands together in a triumphant high five. Mitch thumped me on the back, nearly dislodging my eyeballs. Col grabbed my shoulders and shook me, rattling my teeth. They always did that when Black Baron won a race.

"Jake, that's one champion cockroach," Mitch said.

Rick wagged a finger at me. "Bugsy will take him next time," he promised.

Yeah, right! Who was he trying to kid? Black Baron and Bugsy had raced six times and the record was six to zip the Baron's way. "Yeah," I sneered. "Him and what army?"

I scooped up Black Baron and slipped him into my jacket pocket. He liked it in there. It was dark and warm.

"I gotta go," I said. It was almost dinnertime – for me, anyway. The others had already eaten and were free for the night. My family ate late. We had to wait for Dad to close the deli at 7 pm.

Jimbo gave me his "bummer" look – raised eyebrows and a scrunched-up nose.

I shrugged then headed off, smiling to myself.

Black Baron had won another race, making his record seventeen in a row. He was unbeatable! And it was the end of the school term. No more school for two whole weeks. Heaven!

On the way home I stroked my jacket pocket and gave Black Baron my manager's speech. "Great race, mate. You're in fantastic form. No one can beat you. You're the champ."

An old lady walked past and eyeballed me, like I was some sort of weirdo who talked to himself. I responded with a big, toothy grin. She clutched her handbag and darted along the footpath, like she'd suddenly remembered that she was late for Bingo.

When I got home, I headed straight to my bedroom. I reached under my bed and dragged out an old shoebox. But it wasn't just any old shoebox. It was a mansion fit for a racing legend.

I removed the lid then coaxed the Baron from my pocket. He sat on my finger and looked around. Seeing his Home Sweet Home, he jumped in and settled down for a well-earned rest. As usual, I gave him his favourite treat: a few potato crisps. I ate the rest of the packet.

Black Baron was my second racing cockroach. Pharlap had been my first. He'd shown a lot of promise but he didn't have the guts and dedication of the Baron.

But I'll never know what could have been with Pharlap – he'd met an untimely end. We'd been dog-sitting the pooch next door. Fluffy. What a name! She should have been called Killer or Fang or Jaws the way she disposed of Pharlap with one snap of that steel-trap mouth.

What sort of manager lets his star become dog food … then dog poop? I still cringe at the memory.

And I couldn't utter a word about the killing to my parents or Mrs Saddler, Fluffy/Killer's owner. I never let on about the racing or what was in the shoebox under my bed. My parents would freak. They own a deli, and Dad's always going on about hygiene, germs and stuff. Bugs, especially cockroaches, drive him nuts. He chases them, stomps on them, flattens them with newspapers and sprays them with deadly poisons.

Mum doesn't like crawling critters either. She doesn't scream or yell, like some mothers. She quietly hunts them down and, being the fastest hand in the west with the insect spray, finishes them off without breaking a sweat.

I shudder when I think of them finding Black Baron.

And it isn't just bugs that turn my parents psycho. Mum is a cleaning machine. Seriously! It's her job. She used to work in the deli with Dad, but when business slowed down, she got a job as a cleaner at the local hospital.

She's always on at me about my bedroom. It's the only place in the house with a bit of clutter and mess. It's an oasis in a desert. But she wants to turn my room into an operating theatre at the hospital, all sterile-like.

Last month, I walked into my bedroom and saw Mum's bum sticking out from under my bed. Then I heard a sound that sent a chill through my body.

Mum was humming. She always hums when she's on a cleaning mission. That day she was bashing out the theme from the movie *Mission: Impossible*.

I dashed over to see what she was doing and nearly choked on my tongue when I saw her trying to reach the old shoebox.

"What … what are you doing?" I gasped.

Her reply was muffled. "Cleaning your mess."

"But you can't," I said.

Mum dragged herself out from under my bed.

I let out a long, deep breath. The shoebox was safe, at least for the moment.

Mum had dirt on her nose, cobwebs hanging from her hair and dust balls on her chest. She rubbed her forehead, adding a fresh smear of dirt. "If you cleaned your bedroom, I wouldn't have to."

I don't understand why anyone has to clean my bedroom. I like mess. And I'm sure that mess likes me the way it seems to gravitate towards me.

But I knew better than to argue with Mum when she was in one of her moods. I tried to look sorry even though I felt more like a fish that had been smacked in the head with a baseball bat. "You're right. You shouldn't have to clean my bedroom. I'll do it, I promise, every week."

I had to make that promise. I had to keep her away from Black Baron.

Maybe I gave in too easily because Mum's eyebrows drew together and she gave me this squinty-eyed look, like she had a pain in her head. More like a pain in the neck! Me!

"If you don't clean your bedroom," she said very slowly, as if I didn't understand English, "I'll come in and start chucking stuff out. I don't care what it is. Out it goes. And don't bother asking for a new one."

I nodded, even though I thought she was being ridiculous. Mums don't throw away good stuff, not when it costs *good* money.

So I cleaned my bedroom every week. Okay, I wasn't going to win any awards for being Cleaner of the Year. At least I did it – for a while.

CERTIFICATE
OF MERIT

awarded to
Jake Simpson

for his efforts in
CLEANING
HIS
BEDROOM

But you know how it is? You're good for a short time, while the threat is fresh in your mind, but then it wears off and you lose interest.

Maybe it was my enthusiasm for the holidays. Maybe it was my sense of freedom. Or maybe it was because I didn't believe she was serious, so I didn't think I had anything to worry about. In any case, cleaning was the furthest thing from my mind when I headed to Jimbo's house on the first Saturday of the school break.

I should have taken Black Baron with me. I would have taken him with me if I'd known he was in danger.

If only I'd kept my promise.

CHAPTER 2
A CLEANING FRENZY

It was late afternoon when I left Jimbo's house. It didn't take me long to walk home. He only lives around the corner.

Dad was at the deli for another hour. I was soon to discover that Mum was at home, humming up a storm.

As I walked up the road, I saw something strange in our front garden. I stopped and stared, as if it were something I'd never seen before. Well, I'd never seen one in our front garden, that's for sure!

A bed.

My first thought was that someone must have dumped it there. Not that our front garden looks like a rubbish tip. No, it's perfectly mowed and mulched, pruned and preened.

As I got closer, I realised that the bed was made with a pillow, sheets and a quilt.

Like a semitrailer careening out of control, it hit me. I recognised the quilt and matching pillowcase. It was *my* bed! And it was in our front garden!

Dropping to my hands and knees, I checked under it for an old shoebox.

I saw grass, lots of grass.

Where was Black Baron?

I raced into the house.

I braked when I saw Mum sitting on the couch in the lounge room. In one hand, she held a black garbage bag. In the other hand, she dangled one of my favourite sports shoes by a lace. There was a handful of comics and a can of insect spray on the coffee table.

My stomach churned and threatened to let go of my lunch. "Wha-what's going on?"

"I'm cleaning your bedroom."

She had a funny way of cleaning. She appeared to be tossing away my things, even the good stuff. Especially the good stuff!

That's when I remembered her warning: "If you don't clean your bedroom I'll come in and start chucking stuff out. I don't care what it is. Out it goes. And don't bother asking for a new one."

My mouth fell open. What was I supposed to do without my things? Where was I supposed to sleep? In the front garden?

I was afraid to ask about Black Baron. I was hoping he was still sitting in his shoebox in the empty space where my bed should have been, oblivious to the cleaning frenzy going on around him. Because if he wasn't ...? I gulped. And concentrated on holding down my lunch.

"You obviously weren't doing a very good job of cleaning your bedroom," Mum complained. "There were clothes on the floor, dirty cups on your desk, comics all over the place and a ..." she closed her eyes, like the memory was too horrific, "... a cockroach under your bed."

My heart pounded and I could hardly breathe. Swallowing, I forced out the words, "Was the cockroach in an old shoebox?"

Her eyes fluttered open. "Yes, as a matter of fact it was. It was probably hiding from the filth in your bedroom."

My heart felt like a bomb – tick, tick, tick – any second it would explode. I took a deep breath. "Where is it now?"

"The rotten thing escaped. It was fast. Disappeared out the door before I could whack it." I smiled. Black Baron had beaten Mum, the fastest hand in the west. "We'll have to call an exterminator."

"No!"

Her eyebrows shot up again, like they were spring-loaded. "Do you know something about that horrid thing?"

I sighed and my shoulders sagged beneath the weight of my confession. "His name is Black Baron –"

Birth Certificate

Name:
Black Baron

Date of Birth:
16 January

Place of Birth:
Compost heap at
6 Maryvale Street, Croydon

Mother:
Rosebud

Father:
Felix

Mum's face went into spasms. "His name! His name! It's a dirty, stinking cockroach."

I felt my spine stiffen. Black Baron wasn't an ordinary

cockroach. And he certainly wasn't dirty and stinking. "He's a champ," I argued. "He wins every race."

"Race?" Mum muttered, falling back on the couch and draping one hand over her face. She was quiet for a long time.

I wondered if she'd fainted. I tiptoed to her side and whispered, "Mum, are you all right?"

I saw her mouth twist. Was that normal when you fainted? Early last year, everyone in my class had learnt first aid and received a certificate. But the only thing I remembered was how to save someone from drowning. Should I check Mum's tongue in case she choked on it? Should I turn her head to one side?

"I don't believe you sometimes," she murmured.

I sighed. She wasn't unconscious, which meant I didn't have to save her.

"You know how your father and I feel about bugs." She sat up again. "And you keep a racing cockroach!" she yelled at me so loudly I stumbled backwards.

In the silence that followed we heard a car pull into our driveway.

Dad!

I had to rescue Black Baron before Dad mashed him into the carpet or called an exterminator. Did exterminators work on weekends? Did I have time to save the Baron? I doubted it, knowing how Dad liked to stomp.

There was no time to waste.

CHAPTER 3
WANTED: DEAD OR ALIVE

As I stood looking around my bedroom (or what was left of my bedroom after it had been struck by Hurricane Mum), I felt the urge to call out "Black Baron". But he wasn't a dog or cat that came running at the sound of his name, so I knew it would be pointless. I'd only end up feeling stupid.

Dropping to my hands and knees, I peered beneath my chest of drawers. My heart jumped as I spotted a black shape at the back, near the wall. Was it Black Baron? I frowned as I noticed another dark shape over to the right. Was *that* Black Baron?

I reached for the closest object and dragged it out. As soon as I touched it I knew it wasn't a cockroach. It was too soft and shapeless.

I was right. It was a fluff ball. And it was stuck to my fingers. I flicked it away but it clung to me. I wiped it on the carpet.

Then I reached under the chest of drawers and found the other object. But it was too round and legless to be any kind of bug.

It was an old lid from who-knows-what.

I hurled it at the wall.

Crawling around on the floor, I checked behind the door, in the rubbish bin and under some clothes.

"Where are you, mate?" I asked, then sighed and went to look in the bathroom.

It was easy to see in the bathtub and shower cubicle. Easy to see nothing!

I opened the vanity cupboard. It stank of perfume.

Black Baron wouldn't like it in there. Too smelly. But I checked anyway and spent the next few minutes moving around a load of bottles and jars.

Next, I slithered around on the floor and examined behind the toilet. No grime or germs. No cockroaches or other creepy crawlies.

Biting my bottom lip, I slowly leant over the toilet bowl and checked for floating objects. I smiled. There were some places I was happy to NOT find the Baron.

As I made my way to my parents' study, I heard Dad enter the house. "Why is Jake's bed on our front lawn?" he asked. "And how on earth did it get there?"

Preferring to escape Mum's complaints, I ducked into the study.

"Black Baron," I whispered before I could stop myself.

I shook my head and rolled my eyes. How stupid! He was a cockroach. He wouldn't answer or come running. But he was more than a cockroach to me. He was my mate and a champ.

I peered under the desk. I moved the computer, fax and telephone cords. I looked behind a cupboard but it was impossible to see anything in the thin, dark gap between it and the wall.

The laundry proved just as frustrating.

Even in a house as small as ours, there were too many places for a cockroach to hide.

I was avoiding the kitchen and lounge room. Actually, I was avoiding my parents.

There was only one room left to search down this end of the house: their bedroom. I shuddered at the thought of Black Baron taking refuge in hostile territory.

I heard enemy fire coming from the kitchen.

"He races it!" Dad exploded.

"Can you believe it?" Mum wailed.

I entered their bedroom and hurried to the gap between their bed and the window. Dropping to my stomach, I lifted the bottom of the quilt and peered under the bed. It was getting dark outside but I was afraid to turn on the light, which made it hard to see in the gloomy cavern. I wished I had a torch.

"Where is he?" Dad asked. His voice was getting closer, which meant he was getting closer.

"I don't know," Mum said.

"I'll get changed, call the exterminator, then find that boy."

I grimaced. Dad only called me "that boy" when he was angry.

The light came on. My heart thudded against the carpet. Trying to be as stealthy as a spy, I wriggled under the bed and out of sight.

The slight creak of wood and the soft sighing of the mattress told me Dad had sat down on the bed. I turned my head and saw the bottom of his trousers and his shiny black shoes. He removed his shoes and socks.

Then his trousers dropped to the floor. I turned my head and stared at the curtains. The last thing I wanted to think about was Dad standing there in the nude. Too late! I screwed up my face and shifted my thoughts to something else, like how clean it was under their bed.

"How was work?" Mum asked.

This was no time for conversation, I thought. Couldn't the man get undressed in peace?

"Not bad," Dad said. "Rather quiet near the end of the day."

I heard sounds: the wardrobe door opening, Dad pulling on pants and zipping up.

As I turned my head in his direction, I thought I saw something move. And it wasn't Dad's toes! My heart jerked. Actually my whole body jerked. My hair touching the underneath of the bed made me realise how close I'd come to bumping my head.

I looked around: shadows, carpet, bed legs and wall. Maybe it was the gloom playing tricks on my eyes. Maybe it was wishful thinking. I held my breath, hoping the *something* would move again.

It did. It scuttled closer to the wall near the top of the bed.

A cockroach.

Black Baron.

I grinned.

Now, if only I could reach him …

I stretched my arm up until I felt it straining at the socket but I was still a long way from reaching the Baron. I wriggled my fingers, expecting him to run and jump into my hand. I was his manager. We were a team. But he just sat there, feelers twitching. Then he scurried off, disappearing behind Dad's bedside cupboard.

I couldn't believe it. Was Black Baron angry with me? Did he blame me for his new life as a fugitive? It wasn't my fault.

Okay, so it was my fault. If I'd cleaned my bedroom, like Mum had asked me to, none of this would have happened. Black Baron would be sleeping peacefully

WANTED

DEAD OR ALIVE

BLACK
BARON

in his shoebox or limbering up for his next race. And I wouldn't be hiding under my parents' bed!

Or perhaps the Baron thought we were playing a game – a different kind of training routine. How did I let him know this was deadly serious? It could mean the end of his … um, career. Man, I hoped he stayed out of sight. My stomach churned at the thought of him being so close to Dad.

Speaking of Dad, I hadn't heard him for a while. I hadn't heard him moving around the bedroom nor had I heard him leave.

If he'd gone, then this was my chance to grab the Baron.

Still striving to be as quiet as a cockroach, I slithered from the cavern. I sat up and peeked over the edge of the bed.

Jeez! Dad stood in front of the mirror picking his nose. Oops. Correction. He was doing something with his contact lenses. I stood up. He must have heard me because he stopped, one finger pointing to a green eyeball, like he was going to poke himself in the eye, and stared at me. Actually it was his reflection that stared at me.

I jumped on the bed, because I couldn't think of anything else to do, and lay down as if I didn't have a care in the world. My heart-bomb ticked loudly. His reflection frowned at me. The light bounced off the bald patch in the middle of his black hair, reminding me of the bright lamp used by spies in interrogations. My smile felt like it was glued in place.

He turned around and waggled the finger at me. "I want to talk to you. After I've called the exterminator." He left the room.

CHAPTER 4
RACE TO SAVE BLACK BARON

I was torn between grabbing Black Baron and following Dad.

But I knew finding Black Baron wouldn't be the end of it. My parents would never let me keep him. And there was no point trying to lie about it. Dad was seconds away from calling an exterminator.

I had to make him realise Black Baron wasn't an ordinary cockroach to be stomped on willy-nilly or choked to death with toxic gas. No, he was a champion cockroach. And extermination was murder.

I closed my parents' bedroom door in the slim hope the Baron would still be there when I returned, and followed Dad along the hallway, staring at his stiff shoulders.

"Black Baron is special. Fast. He's won seventeen races in a row. Swifty used to be the champ. His record is seven straight wins." It was a fantastic result. Or so we'd thought at the time.

"Stop calling it that ridiculous name," Dad said. "It's a cockroach. Cockroaches don't have names. They're pests. They spread disease."

When I first started racing cockroaches I'd done some research and I knew Dad was wrong. "Cockroaches aren't dirty. And they only spread disease if the disease is already there."

Turning around, Dad glared at me and held up his hand like a policeman stopping traffic. "I'm not sharing my house with a cockroach as if … as if …" He flung his hands in the air, turned around and stormed off.

Black Baron didn't take up much room, I thought. Besides, no one was using the space under my bed. "He's not hurting anyone," I tried again.

"It isn't natural," Dad said. "People don't keep cockroaches as pets."

"Perhaps they should. Look at all the stray cats that kill native birds. And what about the dogs that are allowed to run wild and poop everywhere?"

It was a good argument, probably my best ever, but Dad didn't let me finish.

"I own a deli. If word got out that my son keeps cockroaches, no one would ever trust my food again. They'd think I tolerate bugs and germs and –" He made a growling sound deep in his throat and grabbed the telephone receiver, almost yanking it from the wall.

"Can't you give me time to find him? *Please*."

I'd been reduced to begging and it made me feel like a real sap. Then I imagined Black Baron's lifeless body, his stiff legs pointing to heaven. I would have thrown myself at Dad's leg and hung on for dear life if I'd thought it would help.

Ignoring me, he dialled a telephone number.

BUG BUSTERS PEST CONTROL

●

Any bug. Any time. All areas.

No job too small. Latest equipment.

No mess. Free quotes.

●

8100 6000

"Yes, I need you to come out today. Right now!"

There was a pause.

"Yes, I know it's late. But I have cockroaches."

A longer pause.

Dad's mouth formed a tight line and his eyebrows drew together. "Monday! You expect me to wait until Monday?"

Sagging against the kitchen wall, I sighed in relief. Monday might give me time to save Black Baron.

"Wait!" Dad said. "Of course I want you to come. I'll see you Monday morning."

He gave the bug murderer our address then hung up. He turned to me. I was trying to slink away. But I wasn't quick enough. I felt his hand on my shoulder.

And so began the lecture. Dad talked about the deli, bugs and germs. He went on about obeying parents, cleaning bedrooms and not wasting time on foolish stuff like cockroach racing. Rather, I could spend more time on homework. Why hadn't I thought of that? It was the usual boring stuff. Don't have fun. Don't have a life. Don't be interesting.

I was grounded for a week. But that didn't bother me too much. My priority was saving the champ.

I rushed to my parents' bedroom but I couldn't

find Black Baron anywhere. I did another check of the house. Even with a torch I couldn't see into some places. I wished I could shrink to the size of a cockroach. Better still, I wished I could find a genie in a bottle and be granted three wishes.

My parents returned my bed to its usual spot. I slipped the empty shoebox underneath, leaving the lid off in case the Baron came home. Then I straightened my bedroom until I barely recognised it.

As I moved about the house, I kept an eye out for the Baron, hoping I'd accidentally find him and wouldn't accidentally tread on him.

Dad must have been looking too. As he walked along the hallway, he suddenly stomped on something. My heart in my throat, I raced to see what it was, but the only black I could find was in the rug's pattern. Another time, he dashed into the toilet, picked up the brush and glared at it. I spotted him staring into corners, pot plants and behind curtains, even up into light fittings. I did the same, hoping to get to Black Baron first.

LOST

A CHAMPION
RACING
COCKROACH,
ANSWERS TO

**BLACK
BARON**

**Ring Jake
any time on**

0514 983 711

Later that night, while watching television, Dad glanced at Mum's shoulder then swept her hair aside to peer at her neck. It gave Mum the creeps. Every now and then, she'd swipe at her neck, like she felt something crawling there.

The next day was Sunday, almost Monday.

When I saw Dad, he looked like he'd slept with one eye open. He had bags the size of potato sacks under his eyes. And his stomping became even wilder (or stranger), like he couldn't see properly.

While making lunch, Mum dropped an olive. It rolled across the floor until Dad stomped on it. My sock got the same treatment. I wouldn't have minded but I was putting it on at the time. Outside, while walking across the front lawn, he suddenly jumped on something small and black (and smelly and messy). He grumbled about bugs and germs as he scraped it off his shoe.

It was a terrible weekend. The worst ever. But I didn't want it to end.

Monday morning came.

Dad rose before the sun and left for the deli, which opened at 7 am. Mum and I got up later. Over breakfast, I decided to make one last appeal.

"Can't we cancel the exterminator? It isn't fair. It's murder."

"You already know the answer to that," Mum said. "I don't like killing any more than you do." It was hard to believe when you saw her wielding the insect spray. "But your father is right. People would stop coming to the deli and we can't afford that. Times are tough enough as it is."

"But what about Black Baron? He can't afford to be dead."

"You should have thought of that before you brought him into this house." She shook her head. "Him! What am I saying? It's a cockroach!"

She was right. I should have left Black Baron at Jimbo's house. He didn't live in an insect war zone like I did.

We had to go out for the day to let the exterminator do his stuff with poison. My original plan, before I was grounded, had involved Jimbo and a comic shop. Mum insisted I went shopping with her so she could keep an eye on me. I wanted to keep an eye on Black Baron. All I could think about was him becoming cockroach compost.

As I was putting on my shoes, I got a brilliant idea. I'd seen those green groups on television trying to save forests by chaining themselves to trees or bulldozers.

I'd chain myself to the kitchen table!

I wasn't trying to save the table. But with me in the house, the exterminator couldn't do his murderous job. Black Baron would be safe!

While Mum was in the bathroom, I slipped outside to the shed and grabbed my bike chain. Returning to the kitchen, I sat on a chair, wrapped the chain around my leg and the leg of the table then locked it. When I moved my leg, I heard the table dragging on the floor as it moved too.

Eventually Mum came out of the bathroom. She walked past me like I was invisible. I moved my leg, rattling the chain and pulling at the table. With a frown, she glanced back at me. Her gaze fell on my chained leg.

"I'm not going anywhere," I said. "I'll die with Black Baron."

CHAPTER 5
THE EXTERMINATOR

Mum slowly shook her head. "It's tempting. Very tempting."

My mouth fell open. How could she say that? I was her flesh and blood, her favourite son. Okay, so I was her only son, only child for that matter. What would she do without me?

"Unlock that thing and hurry up." Mum glanced at her watch. "The exterminator will be here any minute."

That was the whole point. I didn't budge.

Mum sighed. "You're being ridiculous, Jake. All this," she waved her hand at me, "for a dirty cockroach."

"Cockroaches aren't dirty," I pointed out. Again! Cockroaches got such a bad rap. It wasn't fair. If only people would try to understand …

"Ugly. Creepy. Filthy. Useless. Bothersome." She only stopped the insults because the exterminator arrived.

Hearing Mum's words and seeing me chained to the table, the exterminator jumped to the wrong conclusion. "This is a bit drastic, isn't it? Don't worry. They eventually grow out of it. I know. I've got two kids of my own."

I didn't know whether to laugh or be offended.

Mum blushed. "No. This isn't what you think. He's chained himself to the table to stop you killing a stupid cockroach."

Hey! Black Baron wasn't stupid either.

"I see," the exterminator said. But it was obvious he didn't see by the way he looked at me like I was some freak from another planet.

He should look in the mirror! He wore orange overalls with the words:

in black letters across his upper back. He carried a deadly looking machine like the ones I'd seen in science fiction movies about hostile aliens, planet invasions and body snatching.

I was doomed. Black Baron was doomed.

"You have to leave," the exterminator said. "I'll be working with dangerous chemicals." A gas mask hung around his neck, adding to his alien appearance.

"We're just going," Mum said.

"I'm not going anywhere," I repeated.

The exterminator patted his machine like it was a loyal companion. "I kill bugs. Any kind of bug. Big or small. I haven't taken a human life yet."

My mouth felt dry. I swallowed. The way he'd said *yet* made it sound like it could happen one day. Today? I wondered. I felt a bit warm under my arms and around my hairline.

Without another word, the exterminator turned and went outside to his van. I could see him through the kitchen window.

Good, he is leaving, I thought, then frowned. It seemed too easy to get rid of him.

"Jake, I'm getting really tired of this," Mum said.

The exterminator returned with bolt cutters and, before I could stop him, he hacked my bike chain in two.

"Hey!" I looked at Mum. "He's ruined my bike chain."

Mum smiled at the exterminator. "Thank you."

Whose side was she on, anyway?

She grabbed my arm and, with surprising strength, yanked me from the chair then dragged me to the car.

"You'll have to buy me a new bike chain," I grumbled.

She just glared at me, like it was my fault my bike

chain was in pieces.

As we drove to the shopping mall, I looked out the window and tried not to think about Black Baron.

I saw a poster about a car race and a champion driver.

KLIPSOL 500

April 22-26

SEE THE
CHAMPIONS
IN ACTION

FEEL THE POWER

EXPERIENCE THE SPEED

SPECIAL GUEST:
RACING LEGEND PAUL KNOX

Black Baron was a racing champion.

Then I heard an advert for the RSPCA on the radio. I thought about ringing them. Wasn't extermination cruelty to animals?

A bug splattered on our windscreen. I stared at it and sighed. So much for not thinking about the Baron! Everything reminded me of him.

I should have looked after him better. I shouldn't have let him down in the worst possible way. Maybe I shouldn't be a manager to racing cockroaches. I'd killed Pharlap. Well, I hadn't actually killed him. Fluffy/Killer had. But I felt responsible. He'd trusted me and I'd blown it. Just like the Baron.

We arrived at the shopping mall.

"Can I go into Game Zone?" I asked.

Mum gave me a dark look. "You're grounded, remember?"

Wasn't I being punished enough? Obviously not! We went into a dress shop. I shuddered then tried to cloak myself with an invisibility shield. I didn't want anyone to see me.

"Hey!" I heard a familiar voice. Jimbo.

I ducked behind a clothes rack.

"What are you doing?" Jimbo asked, peering down at me.

I quickly told him about Mum's cleaning frenzy, being grounded and the exterminator.

Jimbo's eyes grew big and round. "No way!"

I pulled a face. "We have to save the Baron."

"Yeah. But how?"

I wished I knew. "We have to get back to my place. Did you ride here?"

He nodded. "What about your mum? She'll kill you."

We looked at each other. I could tell we were both thinking about Black Baron.

I checked out the shop. Mum was busy talking to a lady. If I left now, she'd probably ground me forever. But that was nothing compared to what was happening to Black Baron.

"Let's get out of here," I said.

We headed to the door. We were centimetres away from freedom.

"Hello, James."

We froze. Jimbo's face went red. He stared at the floor. "Hi, Mrs Simpson."

Mum stood there holding a shopping bag. "I'm afraid Jake can't see you today or the rest of the week. He's grounded."

"Um, yeah," Jimbo muttered.

"Come on, Jake." Mum put a hand on my back, nudging me forward.

"You go," I whispered to Jimbo.

He looked uncertain.

As Mum and I walked away, I glanced over my shoulder. Jimbo was gone.

I bit my lip and crossed my fingers. I knew there was nothing Jimbo could do. But I wasn't ready to give up. I couldn't.

After the shopping mall, we stopped at the deli to visit Dad. "Did the exterminator arrive?" he asked.

Mum nodded. "Yes. And we had a little incident."

Frowning, Dad glanced at me. I felt a warm prickle run over my skin. It wasn't fair that he jumped to the conclusion I'd caused the so-called incident. Okay, so I had caused the incident, but he wasn't to know that for a fact. It could have been the exterminator. The guy might have had a change of heart and started a Save the Creepy Crawlies Foundation.

SAVE OUR CREEPY CRAWLIES

"What happened?" Dad asked.

"Jake chained himself to the kitchen table and threatened to die with the cockroach."

One of Dad's eyebrows rose. "And you didn't leave him there?"

Very funny! I thought. They didn't know how lucky they were to have a kid like me.

Mum smiled. "I couldn't. Someone might ask questions."

I was about to tell them a thing or two when I saw it. My breath caught in my throat. I blinked, then opened my left eye only to check if it was still there. It was. I closed my left eye and opened my right. Then I slowly opened both.

The tip of a black leg poked out of Dad's jacket pocket.

At work, Dad wore a white jacket, like a doctor, to keep his clothes clean and for reasons of hygiene. Arrghh! I hated that word.

And Black Baron loved jacket pockets.

Of course! Why hadn't I thought of that while I

was searching the house? I should have checked every jacket pocket in the place.

Black Baron was safe from the exterminator. I felt like jumping for joy and sharing a high five with someone.

Then my balloon burst. How was I going to rescue him from Dad's jacket pocket?

CHAPTER 6
THE GREAT ESCAPE

I was surprised Dad hadn't felt a cockroach in his pocket. I was surprised he hadn't smelt it or something. He seemed to have a sixth sense when it came to bugs.

Man, would he freak if he knew what he was carrying around in his jacket. At another time the thought would have split my sides with laughter. But right now I had to save the Baron.

While my parents talked, I planned the great escape. The simplest option was to reach into Dad's pocket and retrieve the Baron. But I didn't like my chances of completing a successful mission. Dad would probably grab my arm and demand to know what I was doing. I could pretend I was brushing away an annoying piece of fluff or something. But I'd been known to walk around for days with twigs, grass and bird poop on my clothes, so my parents were unlikely to believe a bit of fluff or whatever would bother me.

Perhaps I could pretend to help him in the deli – ask to wear his jacket and snatch Black Baron when he wasn't looking?

Or maybe I could offer to take his jacket to the cleaners? But it was so white it almost sparkled; like those perfect teeth in toothpaste commercials.

Unless …

I saw a tiny leg and the tip of Black Baron's nose. Then I saw Dad frown and glance towards his pocket.

There wasn't any time to think about what I was doing. I grabbed a bottle of cola from the drinks fridge, like I'd done hundreds of times. But unlike those times, I turned my back on my parents and shook it vigorously. Then I faced Dad again and unscrewed the lid. A cola volcano erupted, splashing all over Dad and his perfect jacket.

He waved his arms around, as if he could stop the flow of cola with his hands.

I placed the bottle on the counter. It had stopped erupting but a little of the cola dribbled down the side of the bottle onto the counter top.

Dad wiped his face with his hands. He drew his eyebrows together, which reminded me of storm clouds gathering in a thunderous sky. He opened his mouth.

Before he could utter a sound, I mumbled, "Sorry, Dad. The bottle must have been shaken up in the delivery truck on the way here. Let me take your jacket to the cleaners."

Don't get me wrong; I'm not a big fibber. But sometimes a little white lie is necessary to avoid dire consequences. And these consequences could be very dire for Black Baron!

I reached for Dad's jacket but Mum was too quick for me. She dropped her handbag on the floor then grabbed some serviettes. She handed a bunch to Dad and kept a few to help pat him down.

"Get the mop," she said to me. "We don't want anyone slipping in that puddle of drink."

The mop was in the back room. It might as well have been on Mars! "Let me take Dad's jacket," I offered.

"The mop." Mum glared at me.

Now what?

I grabbed some serviettes and began mopping at the pool of cola on the tiled floor. The serviettes immediately became a soggy blob and my hand got soaked. But I didn't care; I was more interested in Mum. She was getting too close to Dad's jacket pocket.

What if I patted down Dad's jacket and grabbed Black Baron at the same time?

"What's that?" Mum shrieked.

My heart pounded and I hoped like crazy she wasn't talking about what I thought she was talking about.

Dad stopped patting himself down. "What's what?"

Mum waved a finger at him. "That black thing in your pocket. I think it had a head."

I jumped up. One foot landed in the pool of cola and slid out from under me. I grabbed the counter top and drinks fridge to steady myself.

"What?" Frowning, Dad fumbled for his pocket. "What sort of head?"

"I don't know," Mum said. "I know it sounds silly but I'm sure I saw something."

I dived at Dad. "Let me take your jacket to the cleaners." We wrestled, becoming a tangle of arms and jacket.

Somehow Dad got his hands free and held me in a vice-like grip. "Not so fast. Let me look at my pocket."

Holding my breath, I prayed Black Baron had escaped during the struggle.

Dad straightened his jacket.

My heart sank. Black Baron, feelers twitching, was perched on the rim of the pocket.

"No!" Dad yelled. "Not in the shop."

Black Baron was used to yelling when he raced. When Dad hollered, the Baron scampered. And I couldn't blame him. He sailed through the air, landing on the floor with the grace of an athlete, and disappeared under the fridge.

Dad clutched his chest. "Call the exterminator before our business is ruined! Lock the doors. Don't let anyone see it."

It was just one teeny-weeny, innocent champion cockroach.

"Is that your cockroach?" Mum demanded.

Now seemed like a good time to get the mop. On second thoughts, Mum looked like she could use it as a weapon.

I shrugged. Well, I didn't know for sure the cockroach in question was Black Baron. It seemed probable, given he was discovered in a pocket.

"I can't believe it! The exterminator is at our house and the cockroach is here."

Dropping to his hands and knees, Dad peered beneath the fridge. He wouldn't have been able to see much because the gap between the fridge and the floor was as thin and dark as a piece of black paper. Next second, he was wriggling around on the tiles like he thought he could slip under the fridge. He wriggled right into the puddle of cola.

"Arrgghh!"

"I thought I told you to mop that up," Mum said, as she picked up the telephone and dialled.

"What if I catch him?" I asked, as I grabbed some serviettes and wiped up what was left of the drink spillage – most of it was now on Dad's jacket. "What if I take him to Jimbo's house?"

Mum hung up the telephone. "The exterminator will be here in twenty minutes."

My stomach felt like a big lump of lead.

I finished cleaning up the cola but the floor was still sticky. I didn't care.

My mobile beeped, letting me know I had a message. I yanked it from my pocket and looked at the text. It was from Jimbo.

No 1 here

He must have been at my house. But the exterminator wasn't there any more. Neither was Black Baron.

Time was running out.

CHAPTER 7
END OF A RACING ERA

I wandered around, searching for Black Baron.

Mum picked up some food and drinks from behind the counter and took them out the back. Dad removed his jacket. His shirt, in places, was damp and dirty. He, too, began marching stuff out the back.

"Jake, grab something and take it out the back to the car," Dad ordered.

Who cared about saving the rotten food?

I wanted to refuse. I wanted to tell him I was too

busy looking for Black Baron. But I was already in a lot of trouble.

If only they didn't own a deli …

If only they weren't such clean freaks …

With a sigh, I grabbed a chunk of ham and a block of cheese.

"Don't use your fingers!" Dad screamed.

This was definitely not my day. Definitely not my week.

I walked slowly, taking the longest route possible to the back of the shop, keeping an eye out for Black Baron.

The exterminator's van screeched to a halt in front of the deli. The man in orange overalls jumped out, grabbed his alien-looking equipment and ran to the door. Mum opened it for him, greeting him like he was a long-lost friend.

During the extermination, I stood outside. The deli windows were plastered with posters advertising all sorts of things.

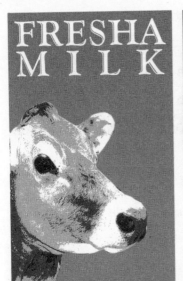

I found a clear spot and pressed my nose against the glass. My guts ached. Wet stuff dampened the window. It must have been raining. Give me a break, all right! So it was my tears dampening the window. I'm tough but I'm not a monster. I'd suffered a great loss. But not as much as Black Baron.

Knowing he'd escaped the poisoning at home and I'd got very close to saving him, only made matters worse.

So I stood there, blubbering like a baby.

I hoped no one saw me. Except for my parents. I wanted them to see my pain, to see how they'd scarred me for life. But they'd gone home, abandoning me in my time of need.

When it was all over, my parents reappeared, paid the exterminator and got on with business as usual.

I entered the deli on shaking legs. I knew what I'd find, and I didn't want to find it. But for some reason I couldn't stop myself. I had to look. I had to know.

There he was, lying on the floor, still and stiff. Poor Black Baron. Taking a deep breath, I gingerly picked him up.

I heard a strange noise, like someone gasping for breath or choking. I looked up and saw Dad gesturing wildly. Mum patted his shoulder and said something I couldn't hear. I sniffed, checking the air for poisonous fumes. It smelt okay to me, and I felt all right. With a frown, I looked around.

I gasped. Then I counted.

There were seven of them. Seven bodies, plus the one in my hand. That made eight dead cockroaches.

I couldn't believe it. Black Baron wasn't the only casualty. No wonder Dad was upset. Eight cockroaches had been living in his spotless, hygienic deli!

Black Baron had been my mate, the champ, but he looked like every other cockroach in the world. I wanted to take him home for an official champion burial but I had no idea which body to bury.

That left me one choice.

I collected all the bodies and pretended to throw them in the bin. Actually, I crammed them in the front pockets of my jeans and took them home. My parents would have killed me if they'd known.

It was awful breaking the news to Jimbo, Col, Mitch and Rick. It was the end of a racing era. The Baron was dead! Long live the Baron.

It was a sombre occasion. A group of us – me, Jimbo, Mitch, Col, Rick and a few others – were gathered around a small hole in the corner of my backyard. We were dressed in our best clothes, hair brushed, faces clean, mouths fresh. It showed how much we thought of the Baron. We didn't scrub up for just anyone.

Carefully I placed a box containing eight bodies into the hole.

"You should say a few words," Jimbo said.

I nodded. "You'll be missed, Black Baron. You were the best. A real champ." I sniffed and my voice wobbled when I spoke again. "I'm sorry about my parents. Rest in peace, mate."

"Peace," Jimbo repeated.

Rick held Bugsy above the grave. "Bugsy wishes he

could be just like you, Black Baron. Not dead, I mean. But, um, a champion. He's never had a better opponent. It's a sad loss for cockroach racing and the world."

Mitch wiped the corner of his eye. "We'll always remember you."

"No one will ever take your place," Col added.

I appreciated their kind words and I was sure Black Baron did too. It was a good send-off, fitting. Starting with me, we all threw two piles of dirt on the box until it was covered.

Then we went inside for a glass of grape juice. We stood around in gloomy silence.

Rick was the first to speak. "What are you going to do now?"

I shrugged.

"Will you get a new cockroach?" Rick asked.

I shook my head. "I don't deserve one, not after Pharlap and Black Baron."

Jimbo touched my shoulder. "Stop beating yourself up. It wasn't your fault."

I disagreed but I didn't bother saying so. They knew how I felt. "I liked racing."

"Yeah," Mitch murmured.

There wasn't much more to say after that, so my friends left me to my misery.

CHAPTER 8
THE LEATHER PRISON

"Stop moping about the house," Mum snapped at me.

"I'm grounded," I reminded her.

"Well, mope in your bedroom where I can't see you," she said. "Anyone would think you'd lost your best friend."

I had.

That night, Dad came home from work with a green budgie in a cage.

"If you want a pet," he said, "this is the sort you

should have."

Black Baron was never a pet. We were a team, a racing legend. But I didn't bother trying to explain that to my parents.

I named the bird Fred. Don't ask me why. It was the first name that popped into my head.

My parents agreed to reduce my grounding to two days, seeing as it was the school holidays, but only if I did a better job of cleaning my bedroom.

Looking after my bedroom wasn't such a big deal, I decided. If for no other reason than if I'd stuck to the job in the first place, Black Baron would still be alive.

Later that night, I was lying on my bed, staring at the ceiling, when Mum stopped in the doorway. "Get your dirty clothes ready. I'm about to do the washing."

After emptying my pockets, I took my dirty clothes to the laundry and shoved them in the washing machine.

"Thank you," Mum said. "Oh, I forgot the sample of fabric softener we got in the letterbox." She smiled.

"Jake, can you grab it from my handbag? It should be in the kitchen."

I found her handbag on the kitchen bench. I opened it and the first thing I noticed was a small packet tucked in the side. Guessing it was the fabric softener, I pulled it out. Something scuttled across Mum's red purse. I dropped the fabric softener.

Leaning forward, I stared inside the bag. It was crammed with a purse, tissues, notepad – all sorts of stuff. And feelers! I saw feelers. My mouth fell open. The feelers were attached to a black body with tiny legs.

Black Baron? What were the chances of finding another cockroach in Mum's handbag? Pretty slim, I thought.

I tried to remember where she'd left it at the deli. She'd dropped it on the floor to help Dad wipe cola from his jacket. She'd dropped it near the fridge.

Man, Mum would freak! Not that she'd ever find out, I decided. I wasn't going to tell her.

I laughed. "Black Baron, it's good to see you."

I coaxed him from his leather prison. He sat on my

palm, feelers twitching. I could tell he was pleased to see me too. I stroked his back.

"I thought you'd been ..." I couldn't say the words. They brought a lump to my throat, even though I now knew the Baron was safe. "I can't believe it!"

"Jake!" Mum yelled. "What's taking so long?"

Mum! In the excitement of finding Black Baron I'd forgotten about Mum and the washing.

"Coming!" I yelled back. But instead of aiming for the laundry, I raced to my bedroom.

"Jake!" Mum called as I sped past the laundry door.

I threw the sample of fabric softener at her. It hit the door and bounced off, landing in the hallway. I didn't stop.

"Thanks," she grumbled. "Sometimes ..."

I'd reached my bedroom and shut the door, so I didn't hear the rest of her words. But I imagined they weren't good.

I slid under my bed and retrieved the shoebox. Even though it was empty and useless, I hadn't been able to throw it away. I placed the Baron inside his home and closed the lid.

A second later, I opened the shoebox again and stared at the Baron. I'd found him in Mum's handbag. Was it enough to convince me this cockroach was Black Baron? I thought about the eight dead bodies.

There was only one sure-fire way to test my suspicions.

I jumped up and headed for the back door, Black Baron in my jacket pocket.

"Where are you going?" Mum asked. "You're grounded."

"I'm only going outside," I explained. "And I'll be staying in our yard."

It was true. Okay, so I'd left out a few minor details, like what was in my pocket and why I was going outside.

I walked to the bottom of the driveway, because it was a great place to race a cockroach and also because my parents couldn't see me from the house.

My heart pounded and, though I was warm enough, I felt kind of shivery inside. I placed the cockroach on the concrete and took a deep breath. "Ready. Go!"

Off he went, like he'd done dozens of times before. He was fast. A winner. The Baron was back!

I couldn't wait for the next race.

CHAPTER 9
LONG LIVE THE CHAMP

I had to wait until my grounding was over and I was a free man again. Another day went by. So many times I wanted to call and tell Jimbo about Black Baron. But for some reason, I decided to keep it a secret and surprise him at the next race.

Eventually, I was able to get everyone together. Soon they'd all know. Well, at least the small crowd that had gathered around Jimbo's driveway.

Too much grinning over the past couple of days had given me a face-ache.

"I thought you weren't getting another cockroach," Jimbo said.

I shrugged. "He sort of found me."

Jimbo frowned. "What do you mean?"

I didn't answer. When Black Baron won, I'd tell them what I knew about the greatest escape ever.

Jimbo shook his head. "I should have known you weren't serious. What's his name?"

"Let's just call him Champ for now."

Jimbo laughed. Then he said, "Take your places."

Rick and I crouched at the start line – the top of Jimbo's driveway – and held onto our competitors in readiness for the big event.

"Is he as good as Black Baron?" Rick asked.

I smiled. "There's only one Black Baron."

Rick slowly nodded.

"Ready." Jimbo paused, letting the tension build. My insides twisted and crawled, like they were infested with bugs. "Go!"

The race was on!

"Come on, Bla– boy," I called.

"Hurry up, Bugsy," Rick yelled. "You can do it."

But Bugsy was struggling as he always did against the Baron. Black Baron didn't seem to be trying but he was miles ahead.

LONG LIVE THE CHAMP

A roar went up as Black Baron crossed the finishing line.

Jimbo and I slapped our hands together in a triumphant high five. Mitch thumped me on the back, nearly dislodging my eyeballs. Col grabbed my shoulders and shook me, rattling my teeth.

I grabbed Black Baron. "Good one, mate. Eighteen

in a row."

Jimbo peered at me like I'd suddenly grown two heads. "What are you doing? That's Black Baron's record. You can't –"

I laughed. "I can. Because this little beauty is Black Baron."

"But we buried the Baron," Col reminded us.

"We *thought* we buried the Baron," I corrected him.

Mitch shrugged. "We buried eight cockroaches."

"How did he survive?" Jimbo asked. "Where did you find him?"

"I found this guy in Mum's handbag. He must have climbed in there while we were waiting for the exterminator. Then Mum took her handbag home. That's how he missed being exterminated."

I didn't know that for a fact but it was the best explanation for his miraculous survival. He'd beaten the exterminator not once, but twice. What a champ!

"You've seen him race. He's fast. Because he's Black Baron."

Jimbo smiled. "That's amazing."

I nodded. "I know. The Baron is invincible!"

"Fantastic!" Mitch exclaimed.

"Long live the Baron," Col added.

"What about your parents?" Jimbo asked. "If they find out Black Baron is still alive …" He didn't need to finish the sentence. We all knew what he meant.

"He can't live at my place," I agreed. "It's too risky."

"I could look after him," Jimbo offered.

"Looking after a champion racing cockroach is a big responsibility," I said.

"Don't worry." Jimbo patted me on the back. "Mum doesn't know one end of a vacuum cleaner from the other."

Yeah, I'd always liked Jimbo's mum. But I had another idea.

CHAPTER 10
COCKROACH HEAVEN

We stood at the rubbish dump – me, Jimbo, Col, Mitch and Rick.

BEVERLEY RUBBISH DISPOSAL

Keeping our suburbs clean

OPENING HOURS:
Weekdays 8 am-7 pm   Weekends 8 am-12 pm

"You're doing the right thing," Mitch said.

I nodded. So why did I feel so hollow inside?

Squatting down, I placed the old shoebox on the ground. I removed the lid then reached in and picked up Black Baron. I didn't mean to hold him for so long. Jimbo put his arm around my shoulder. I swallowed against the lump in my throat.

I let the Baron go. Rick let Bugsy go. The two cockroaches raced away, with Black Baron in the lead.

The Baron stopped and waved a feeler at me. Then he disappeared beneath a pile of rubbish.

I smiled and looked around at the miles and miles of rubbish. Now the Baron was truly in cockroach heaven!

GOING FOR BROKE

Nathan Foley is desperate for greatness.

Record-breaking greatness.

Planning? Who needs it?

Research? What's that?

Nathan's on a path to glory.

What could go wrong?

MORE LIGHTNING STRIKES!

A sneak peek of
'GOING FOR BROKE' by Meg McKinlay

CHAPTER 1
DORKFACE GETS A PLAN

It's Josh Tuttle dropping his trophy on my foot at the end-of-term assembly that finally makes my mind up.

It's not all his fault, though. He's just the last straw, the last amazing genius in an assembly full of kids doing fantastic, unbelievable things.

Apart from being so all-round wonderful and talented, these kids all have one thing in common.

They are not me.

The official theme for the assembly is "Young

Achievers", but it might as well be "Everyone In This School Is Way Better Than You, Dork-Face".

First, it's Janie Parsons and her robotic dog. That thing can roll over, beg, and fetch a newspaper. It's a marvel of modern science, built entirely from tin cans and parts from a radio she found at the rubbish tip.

Mr Stipanov, the principal, applauds so hard he almost falls over. Then he gives Janie a little crystal ball on a gold stand. She's a Young Scientist of the New Millennium.

Next, it's Anthony Jenkovic and his black belt in every martial art you've ever heard of. And some you haven't. Which I suspect he might have actually made up himself.

Mr Stipanov fake karate chops him, and hands him a shiny plaque in the shape of a clenched fist, covered in Japanese writing. Anthony, he says, is a Butt Kicker for the Modern Age.

Okay, he doesn't exactly say that. But that's what he means.

Then it's maths geniuses and junior sports stars

and kids who play chess on weekends. There's even a Year One kid who scored a part in *Neighbours*. His job is to point at a sports car and say "Coool!" The whole school goes wild for him. Girls in Year Seven want his autograph.

The kid is six years old. He probably doesn't even know how to write. For all I know, it took him twenty-seven takes to get that one word right. For all I know, they ended up dubbing it in later.

It doesn't matter. He's a star.

And I'm sitting on my bum on a piece of ratty carpet square while Year Seven kids flick spitballs at me from behind.

Finally, it's Josh Tuttle, breaking the State Record for the 800 metres. He fist-pumps the air as he walks up to collect a trophy that's almost as tall as he is.

I clap along with everyone else, because Mrs Cheval is watching, then I turn to Weasel Burton, who's grinding his teeth next to me.

"Is it just me," I say, "or are there way too many high achievers at this school?"

Weasel grins, and jabs me in the side again. So far, he's managed to wind me five times without Mrs Cheval noticing once.

Now *that's* talent.

I shuffle my bum around on my piece of carpet; it's so frayed it hardly keeps me off the cold concrete now. But that's probably because I spend every assembly picking at the loose threads when I'm bored, which is all the time.

There's only so much basking in other people's glory you can take.

At least this one's nearly over. All that's left is for Mr Stipanov to make a short speech about the amazing amazingness of all the kids lined up on the stage. He'll say "Well, children" and "real credit to the school" about sixteen times. Then the photographer from the local paper will take photos and write an article about the incredible talent and skill of all the kids who aren't me.

Shouldn't be long now.

Oh, wait.

There's one more thing.

"*Well, children*, it seems that last assembly we left one student, who is also a *real credit to the school*, out of the merit awards."

This is *terribly unfortunate*, apparently. Mr Stipanov is falling over himself to apologise.

Weasel digs me in the ribs again, snickering. According to Mr Stipanov, some "cheerful lad" has won a small rectangle of red cardboard for being "a kind-hearted and thoughtful classmate".

Sucked in to that kid.

Last year, I won mine for "writing a very interesting narrative recount". Go ahead, ask me. I have no idea what a narrative recount is. I did write a note to Weasel about the time Dad backed the car into a tree, so maybe that was it.

The point is, it doesn't matter. Everyone knows you win one merit award a year, no matter how much you suck. You could sit in a corner farting all year and they'd still find something for you.

CERTIFICATE OF MERIT
awarded to
Wendell Burton
for Consistent Commitment
To Gas Production
Wendell Is A Conscientious
Consumer Of Baked Beans.
Keep up the good work, Wendell!
Mrs Cheval

There's a scattering of no-one-really-cares applause and then someone pokes me in the side.

"Go on!"

I look up from picking at my carpet square. From the non-Weasel side, Ronnie Symons is waggling his eyebrows, and Mrs Cheval is leaning down the row, hissing at me.

That's when I play back Mr Stipanov's announcement in my head, and my whole body goes cold.

" … this extra special end-of-term assembly merit award goes to … Nathan Foley."

Being me.

Ronnie and Weasel push me forward and I stumble up and out of the line, and start the long, slow march down the centre of the aisle. I keep my eyes focused on Mr Stipanov and his tiny square of red cardboard, and try not to be blinded by the flashes of gold and polished metal behind him on the stage.

Mr Stipanov leans forward, beaming, and shakes my hand. "Well done, son. Nothing like being a cheerful lad."

I turn to walk back to my place, but he waves me up onto the stage "with our other prize-winners". I squeeze in next to Josh Tuttle, my craptacular square of cardboard behind my back, and that's when it happens.

They should have seen it coming, really. Because Josh Tuttle, in spite of all his amazing amazingness, is not that big. He's one of those wiry, zippy guys who slips past you in a race like the air's opening up to let him through. He's the guy you don't see coming until he's whizzed past your ear.

As I watch him lose his grip on the trophy, and see it toppling towards me, I think how much better it would have been if they'd just given him a square of cardboard.

The edge of the trophy's base comes down hard on my foot.

A camera flashes, catching me mid-*auuuughhhh!*, and this is the picture that will appear in the school newsletter tomorrow. If you look closely at my flailing hands, you'll be able to make out the smiley-face stickers on my merit award.

I stumble backwards into the row of kids behind me. Luckily, they're all legends of martial arts and various other sports, and they brace themselves against me, blocking my fall.

From the wings, Mr Marshall, the caretaker, lunges onto the stage and grabs the trophy. He pulls it back towards him, using my foot as a pivot point.

In the crowd, Ronnie and Weasel are grinning, doing a long, slow handclap all on their own.

Mr Marshall glares at me, and escorts Josh to the other end of the row. For the rest of the assembly, he acts as Josh's own personal trophy-holder.

"I think my toe is broken," I say, to no one in particular.

"Shut up, Foley," replies someone behind me, so I do. I stand there with my throbbing toe, my square of red cardboard shoved into my back pocket. I'll get in trouble for that later, when it's time for the newspaper journalist to smirk and put me in the centre of his "junior champions" photo spread, but I'm not thinking about that now.

I'm watching Weasel point at me and mouth the word "high achiever" over and over while silently cacking himself.

And I'm working out a foolproof, ingenious plan for becoming amazingly amazing. For getting up on stage, in the paper even, without a broken toe and a really lame square of red cardboard.